Christmas Magic

igloobooks
.com

I'm bursting to tell you about Christmas and why it's so much fun.

It's the sparkliest, jingliest time of year and I can't wait for it to come.

Daddy will get the Christmas tree and put it up in the hall.

I'll cover it with fairy lights and sparkly glittering balls.

I'll help my mum in the kitchen with the delicious things she'll make,

Like sticky, sweet mince pies and a scrummy Christmas cake.

I'll write my note to Santa, but I always change my mind.

I'm sure Santa won't be cross though, I think he's very kind.

Carol singers will ring the bell and sing outside our door.

When they've sung their songs, I'll ask, "Can you sing some more?"

There'll be Christmas cards to all my friends, stuck with glitter and glue.

Look out when the postman comes, there might be one for you!

I'll throw snowballs at my brother, they'll go whoosh and thud and splat!

We'll laugh and make a snowman and he'll wear Daddy's hat.

I'll pretend my toys are reindeer and I am Santa on my sleigh.

I'll load my sack with presents and then I'll fly away.

Mum will read me stories and tell tales of Christmas past.

Then when the fire goes out, it will be time for bed at last.

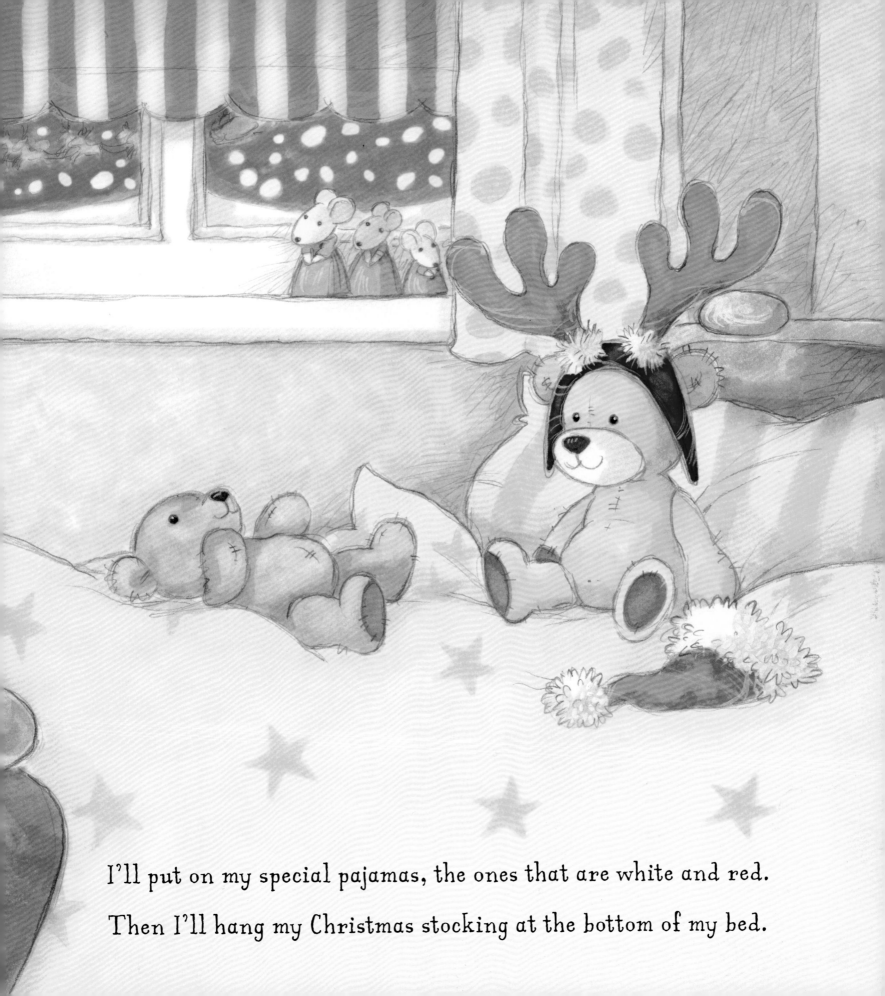

I'll put on my special pajamas, the ones that are white and red.

Then I'll hang my Christmas stocking at the bottom of my bed.

When I'm fast asleep, Santa will fly to visit me.

He'll wriggle down the chimney and leave presents under the tree.

I won't sleep I'll be so excited, because Christmas is loads of fun.

In the morning, I'll run downstairs and shout,

"Merry Christmas, everyone!"